Rafters

The
Adventure Begins...

D1147570

by Nilsson Hennelly
illustrations by T. Runnells

A ROXBURY PARK BOOK

LOWELL HOUSE JUVENILE

LOS ANGELES

CONTEMPORARY BOOKS

CHICAGO

Dedication

For my beloved grandmother, Ella Dorothea Christiane

Rafters was created by Roxbury Park

Roxbury Park is an imprint of Lowell House,
A Division of the RGA Publishing Group, Inc.

Requests for such permissions should be addressed to:

Lowell House
2020 Avenue of the Stars, Suite 300
Los Angeles, CA 90067

Lowell House books can be purchased at special discounts
when ordered in bulk for premiums and special sales.
Contact Department TC at the above address.

Publisher: Jack Artenstein
Editor in Chief, Roxbury Park Books: Michael Artenstein
Director of Publishing Services: Rena Copperman
Managing Editor: Lindsey Hay
Text design: Bret Perry
Cover illustration by: Warren Chang

Library of Congress Cataloging-in-Publication Data

Hennelly, Nilsson.
 Rafters / by Nilsson Hennelly.
  p. cm.
"A Roxbury Park book."
 Summary: When thirteen-year-old Jack and his older brother
Ben are given a special rubber raft by a mysterious man at the fair,
they travel on the river through a vortex into a strange new world,
where Ben disappears.
  ISBN 1-56565-947-3
  [1. Fairs—Fiction. 2. Brothers—Fiction. 3. Space and
  time—Fiction] I. Title.
  PZ7.H39133Raf 1998
[Fic]—dc21   98-18026
                                                        CIP
                                                        AC

Manufactured in the United States of America

691439

10 9 8 7 6 5 4 3 2 1

1

~~~~~~~~~~~~~~~~~~~~~~~~~~~~~~~~~~~~~

J ack!" Mom screamed. "It's nine o'clock. Get out of bed and help your brother in the yard. JAAAAAAAACK!"

I wanted to answer my mother, honestly. And a part of me wanted to help my brother paint the fence, too. But it must have been a very small part of me—too small to convince the rest of me to get out of bed.

Just a few more minutes of sleep, I told myself. Like every other night that August, the heat and humidity had made sleeping through the night almost impossible.

"Jaaaaaack!" Mom yelled. I heard her shoes squeaking down the wooden staircase. When the screen door wheezed open, I lowered myself down from the top bunk bed and shuffled over to the window facing the street just in time to see Mom's white nurse's uniform disappearing into our Toyota Corolla.

Through the open window I saw my older brother, Ben, kneeling on the sidewalk below. He was adding a fresh coat of white paint to our fence. He waved as Mom pulled the car out of the driveway and slowly drove away. When he saw me, he thrust a dripping paint brush in the air.

"Hey, Jack!" he yelled. "How about giving me a hand with the fence." There were splotches of white paint in his black curly hair. His favorite blue T-shirt was also spattered with paint.

Ben was fifteen, only three years older than me, and more responsible than other boys

his age. I wondered how long he'd been out-side painting. Even during summer vacation Ben woke up every morning at six, and went downstairs to do some chore or to exercise. He sometimes asked me to join him, but I always declined as a matter of principle. For me, sum-mer meant looking for thrills and adventures around every corner, and sleeping *late.*

Ben hasn't always been so responsible. Everything changed last year when Dad died in a car accident. I guess, in a way, Ben feels like he has to be my brother and my father. Believe me, I understand how difficult it is just being my brother, let alone my father, too.

"Well?" Ben yelled. "Are you coming?"

I rubbed my eyes with my fists. "I'll be right down."

After brushing my teeth and washing my face, I put on a pair of shorts and a shirt, grabbed a couple of dollars from my top dresser drawer, and ran downstairs.

In the kitchen I poured myself a small glass of orange juice, then grabbed a slice of bread from the pantry. As I chewed on the slice of dry bread, I looked at the photographs on the phony brick wall beside the refrigerator. There were pictures of Mom, Ben and Mom, Mom and Me, Mom's parents—everybody but Dad. All the pictures of Dad disappeared from our house right after the accident.

I put the empty glass in the sink, wiped the sweat from my forehead, and walked back into the hallway.

Through the screen door I saw Ben stirring a fresh can of paint. Already the temperature was scorching hot. *Would it ever let up?* I pressed my nose against the screen and looked at the neighborhood where I'd spent my whole life, imagining how it might look to an outsider.

Not exactly Beverly Hills.

Dunmoore hadn't changed much over the years. The small houses up and down River Road were all in various stages of neglect. Some lawns had not been mowed in years. They looked like miniature jungles. Others had broken-down cars parked in the front yard. There was even an abandoned house a few doors down where the Coles used to live. About six months ago, Mr. Cole got a promotion, and the family moved practically the next day. Most of the windows in the house had been smashed. A sign for the County Fair had even been planted on the front lawn. It read: *Come to the Dunmoore County Fair (August through September) and experience the fun and excitement of a lifetime!*

I've been living in Dunmoore County since I was born. If I had to choose two words to describe my life here, they would probably not be *fun* or *excitement*.

I don't know what got into me, but suddenly the thought of walking through the front door made my stomach turn. I backed up a few feet and turned to look down the hallway in the other direction—toward the open back door. The woods behind our house were drenched in bright sunlight. It was probably cool in the shade under the trees—much cooler than the front yard. About fifty feet beyond the fringe of the woods was the Dunmoore River. The fairgrounds were only a fifteen-minute walk along the river through the woods.

Eight minutes if you ran.

"Jack!"

Startled, I turned around to see Ben standing right outside the front door.

"What are you doing?" he asked suspiciously.

I took another step toward the back of the house, then another. "Uh, I have to go out for a while . . . "

"Jack!"

"Leave part of the fence for me, Ben. I'll be back by lunchtime, I promise."

Ben wiped paint onto his pants and pushed open the screen door. "I know where you're going, Jack. I'll catch you and drag you back here . . . I swear. . . ."

"No you won't!" I cried, and sprinted for the back door.

I've always been a fast runner. I reached the path in the woods in a flash and slowed down to look over my shoulder. Ben was nowhere in sight.

I felt kind of bad leaving him behind to do all the work alone. But the truth is, I honestly planned to do my share of the painting . . . just on my own terms, which meant later.

Right now I had a fair to go to.

2

onald Lipton swept the quarters into a slot on the end of the wooden counter. "No winners. No winners," he said in a voice that cracked every few syllables. The arrow on the giant spinning wheel had come to rest on the name *Anne-Marie.* I had chosen the name *Clarence,* which was about seventy names away on the huge wheel. I looked down greedily at the prizes stacked up around the wheel. There was everything from a toaster to stuffed animals to compact disks.

Dejected, the other three players walked away from the booth and headed off in different directions.

"Step right up," Ronald yelled. "Place a quarter on the right name and win a prize!"

But nobody was listening. The few people who'd come to the fair this early were busy riding the Ferris Wheel or screaming in the haunted house. Dejected, Ronald sighed and pulled over a wooden stool to sit on.

"It's dead around here, man," Ronald complained. He picked up a crumpled copy of *Sports Illustrated for Kids* and began to fan himself. Ronald was my best friend. We met our first year in Little League, and have been hanging out together ever since. Each year, Ronald's dad took us to a Twins game, and each year—at least so far—the Twins lost. Ronald's father was also one of the people in charge of running the fair. Lucky Ronald got to work at whatever booth or

concession stand he wanted. Last year it was the basketball hoop.

The only bad thing about Ronald's working at the fair was that we hardly ever got to hang out during the day.

"So how did you get out of painting the fence?" he asked, handing me another quarter from his coin belt. I placed it on the name *Mort.*

"Oh, that," I said. "I'm going to do it later, when I feel like it. Besides, it's way too hot now." I wiped my forehead with my sleeve for effect.

Ronald reached under the counter and pressed a button that started the wooden arrow clicking around the board. "Dude, you watch the Twins game last night?" he asked, sticking a toothpick between his teeth.

"I listened to it on the radio."

"Man, they stink," Ronald said.

"Really."

We both watched as the arrow slowed down and clicked for the final time on the name *Milton.*

I said, "I've been here for almost two hours and I haven't come close to guessing the right name once. Has anybody ever won this game?"

"Nope." Ronald pulled the toothpick out of his mouth. "It's more likely to happen at night, though, when it's crowded and more people play."

"Hello, Jack Pierce."

I recognized the voice immediately. It belonged to Keiko Ozawa, my least favorite neighbor. She was standing next to a girl I'd never seen before. I turned around and forced a smile. "What's going on, Keeko."

"It's pronounced *cake-oh,*" she corrected me, folding her arms across her chest.

"Whatever."

"I can't believe you don't know that by now."

Actually, I *did* know how to say her name. I'd sure heard it enough lately. Six months ago, Keiko had moved in with her grandparents, who lived down the street from us. I couldn't stand her. She was always hanging around Ben, giggling and agreeing with everything he said. Keiko was only thirteen, but she tried to act older to impress Ben. It drove me nuts.

I tried to avoid her whenever possible.

"So, Jack, paint any fences recently?" Keiko continued, smiling at her friend. "I ran into Ben a few minutes ago," she said. "I'd say he was definitely pissed off. Wouldn't you agree, Sue?"

The other girl chuckled. "Definitely."

I turned to Sue. "What are you laughing at?"

Sue looked down. Keiko asked, "So, when is Ben going to get here?"

My heart skipped a beat. "Ben's not coming here."

A smile crept over Keiko's face. "Really? That's not what he just told me." Keiko's smile widened as she placed a hand on her friend's shoulder. "Let's go, Sue. There are so many *interesting* things to do here. Bye guys." Keiko laughed as she and her friend walked down the dirt aisle toward the Ferris Wheel.

Ronald shook his head. "That's harsh, man."

"I'm going," I said.

"No rides today?" Ronald asked.

"Those rides bore me. I've already been on the mini-coaster twelve times, the salt-and-pepper shakers, ten, the Ferris Wheel, eight, and the Twister, five. And you know what? I might as well have been lying in bed, sleeping. That's how boring they were." I put my hands on my hips and puffed out my cheeks. "I don't know, Ron. I don't think there's a ride out there exciting enough for me."

"Cool," Ronald said.

"Anyway, I'll catch you later."

I decided to get something to drink before I headed back, but when I started toward the nearest refreshment stand, I saw something that made the hair on the back of my neck stand up.

I stopped cold in my tracks. Standing about fifty feet away and facing me on the dirt path was an old man, maybe seventy or eighty, staring at me with crazy, bulging eyes. Tall and stooped over, with scraggly long hair, the old man wore an old-fashioned black suit and a white bow tie. I wanted to run away, but it was like his eyes were glueing me in place. He was so creepy, I thought I was going to pass out. He just stood there glaring at me!

Suddenly a hand slammed down on my shoulder. I jumped, turned around, and saw Ben standing over me. "Oh, it's you," I said, breathing a sigh of relief. I looked up at him,

trying to think of what to say. Then I remembered the old man, but when I turned around, he was gone. *Weird,* I thought.

Ben had his hands on his hips. "All right, let's go."

"Where are we going?"

Ben shook his head and frowned. "I can't believe you just ran off, Jack. You know we have to finish painting the fence. Did you expect me to do it by myself?"

Ben's hand was still gripping my shoulder when we started walking back. I said, "I'm sorry. I know I shouldn't have taken off like that. But I was going to come back to help you, honest. I just had to get out of there. It's that house, Ben. Sometimes I feel like the walls are going to cave in on me. Do you know what I mean?"

Ben rolled his eyes. "We were supposed to work *outside*, Jack. In the front yard, where there are no walls."

I shoved my hands in my pockets. "I saw Keiko earlier," I announced. It seemed like a good time to talk about something else. "I think she's in love with you."

My brother stopped walking. "Look, if you're trying to change the subject, it's not going to work. Besides, Keiko's not in love with me. We're just friends."

"Yeah, sure."

I have to admit, I had no doubts about what would happen next.

In a flash Ben was chasing me, pumping his arms and shouting, "Get back here, Jack. You'll never get away!"

"Oh, yes I will," I yelled back. I was running as fast as I could run, weaving through the thin crowds and laughing. Ben was laughing, too. I felt like I could run fifty miles without stopping. I closed my eyes and imagined myself flying through wispy clouds high in the sky.

I never saw Arty Buller. I only heard him. "Ahhhhhh!"

My head rammed into his big stomach and we both tumbled into a stack of hay outside the horse shed.

Arty got up first. A long piece of hay hung from one nostril. His face was red with anger and his breathing was heavy and laborious. "Let's go, Pierce." Arty held his hands in front of his face like a boxer. "You throw the first punch, so I can knock you out."

"Are you guys all right?" Ben walked up between us, and immediately Arty lowered his guard.

"Yeah," grumbled Arty. "I guess."

I tried my best not to snicker. Arty was the neighborhood bully. He specialized in picking on kids who were younger and smaller than he was. Arty was Ben's age, but he was short and fat, without a trace of muscle. Ben played football on the high

school junior varsity team. Guys like Ben scared guys like Arty. I moved behind Ben and, against my better judgment, gave a quick sneer.

I swear I could see Arty's short blond hair bristle with anger. He lifted up his arm and pointed at me. "I'll get you, Pierce. Just wait 'til your big brother isn't around to save you." He turned and stomped away.

"Are you okay?" Ben asked.

"Yeah. I'm just glad you were here. If you weren't, I might have really hurt him."

Ben smirked and turned toward the exit. Before I followed him, I turned back to look at the fairgrounds once more. With all the excitement I'd forgotten about the strange old man with the long white hair. I wondered who he was, and if I'd ever see him again.

3

That night, while we sat at the dinner table, I asked Mom if she would loan me a few dollars.

"What do you need it for?" she asked.

I swallowed a mouthful of juice. "There are a couple of books I'd like to buy."

Ben rolled his eyes and speared a few green beans with his fork.

Mom wiped her mouth, stood up, and walked over to the kitchen sink. "Why didn't you two finish painting the fence?"

"Uh . . ." I looked across the table at Ben.

"We wanted to finish today, Mom, but we ran out of paint," Ben explained. "I didn't realize we had more cans in the basement. We'll finish tomorrow, I promise." He stared at me grimly.

Mom turned around and faced us. She was drying a glass with a dish towel. "When you finish the fence, I'll give each of you ten dollars. Not until then."

"But couldn't we have the—"

"Not one minute sooner," Mom said sharply.

When she leaned over to pick up the carton of juice, I noticed how much older she looked compared with just a year ago. Her dark hair was mixed with streaks of gray and the wrinkles in the corners of her eyes and her forehead seemed longer and deeper.

"Tomorrow I'm working a double shift at the hospital," Mom said. "I have an hour

break at ten o'clock. If I have time, I'll come home to make sure you two are okay."

"You don't have to come home, Mom," Ben said. "I can take care of everything."

Mom put one hand on Ben's head and the other on mine. "I really appreciate you guys. You know that, right?"

Ben smiled weakly. He looked like he was going to cry, the way he sometimes did when Mom got emotional. Since Dad died, Mom and Ben have gotten really close. Sometimes I hear them crying together in the morning before I get up. Me, I cried a little bit at Dad's funeral, but not since then.

That night I sneaked Dad's old transistor radio into bed with me. The Twins were playing in California, so the game started late, about ten.

"What's that sound?" Ben asked. He was lying on the lower bunk bed. "Do you have that radio on?"

I shoved the radio under my pillow and clicked off the switch. "No," I lied. The rule was no radios—no nothing—after 10:00 P.M. It was quiet for a few minutes. From across the room the electric fan on Ben's desk rattled, blowing hot air toward us.

Even with the windows open the temperature in our room was super hot. We had an air conditioning unit downstairs but it was too expensive to turn on. I could hear Ben squirming around below me.

"It's so hot!" he hissed.

I turned on my side and said, "Ben, do you remember when we were little, when Mom and Dad used to take us down to the river to go swimming when it was really hot?"

"Yeah. We went at night a few times, too. It's hard to imagine the four of us swimming in the river at night, isn't it?"

"Actually, it wasn't the four of us," I said. "Dad never went in the water."

"Well, you know what I mean. At least we were all there, together." Ben turned on his other side. "Jack, do you think maybe you're angry about what happened to Dad? I remember feeling that way right after he died."

"I'm going to listen to the Twins game."

Ben cleared his throat. I knew what was coming. Almost every time Dad came up, Ben gave me the same speech. I could have said it for him.

He said, "Jack, school starts in a couple of weeks. Why don't you at least talk to the counselor . . . you know . . . about Dad. I did, and it made me feel a lot better. And you know it would make Mom happy."

There was silence, then Ben continued. "Look, I'm not Dad. I know that. But I think in this case I know what's good for you. So why don't you give it a shot?"

I swung my arms behind my head and sighed. "I already told you and Mom. I don't

need to talk to anybody about Dad. I'm not just saying that, either. It's the truth. I don't even think about Dad anymore!"

It took a few seconds before I realized what I'd said. It sounded awful, but it was the truth. For me, Dad was becoming a distant memory. But I didn't mean to hurt Ben's feelings. Maybe I shouldn't have shared that truth with him. Anyway, I began to feel sort of guilty about the whole thing, so I said, "Well, if you think it's a good idea . . ."

Ben sat straight up. "Really? That's great, Jack. Mom will be really happy."

"There's just one condition," I said. "We have to go fishing or swimming tomorrow. At the river, like the old days."

Ben was quiet for a moment. "Jack, you know Mom doesn't want us swimming in the river. It's too dangerous. Remember what happened to Angela Aims?"

"Angela fell through the ice, Ben. In the winter. It's not exactly the same thing."

Ben squirmed around on his bed and yawned. "After we finish painting the fence, we'll do something, okay?"

It was better than nothing. Besides, I had plenty of time to get out of seeing the counselor at school.

I said, "Yeah, I guess."

Ben reached across his bed and turned off the lamp on the night table.

In the corner of the room, the electric fan rattled on. Even at night, the heat was heavy and damp. I closed my eyes and tried to imagine a snowy winter day.

In less than five minutes Ben was snoring like a bear. I pulled the radio out from under my pillow and switched on the Twins game, but my mind kept drifting. I looked out the window facing the backyard. The edge of the forest was like a huge black curtain,

concealing the river and all its mysteries. I closed my eyes and pictured a family playing in the shallow water near the river bank. Silver moonlight streamed down from gaps in the tall trees, and I could see Ben, Mom, and me laughing and splashing one another.

I looked on the bank where Dad was sitting, but his chair was empty.

4

We finally finished painting the fence the next day, but not until four o'clock in the afternoon.

"I thought this would never end," I said. My arms and legs were aching me so much, I lay down on the sidewalk and didn't move. My T-shirt was soaked through from the heat, which was even worse than the day before.

"Don't you feel good?" asked Ben triumphantly. "Doesn't it feel good to accomplish something?"

He was standing by the fence, holding a paint brush in his hand like it was the Olympic torch. I was beginning to think that something was wrong with my brother.

"Do you want to go to the fair, Jack?"

I sat up just as Ben pulled something out of his pants pocket. It was a ten dollar bill. "Yeah," I said. "But what about a swim?"

"Maybe later," Ben said unconvincingly. Suddenly, he seemed distracted.

I never saw the purple bicycle coming up behind me.

"Hey, guys," Keiko Ozawa said.

Nightmare! I buried my head in my hands.

Keiko rode her bike right up to Ben. "What are you guys doing?"

Ben shoved his hands in his pockets. I prayed for him to lie. "Well," he started to say. "Uh . . ." He glanced in my direction. "We were just about to go to the fair. . . . Do you want to come?"

Now, let's get something straight: I don't hate girls—well, only one girl—and I can prove it. One of my best friends at school is a girl. Elizabeth Winslow is one of the coolest people I know. We've been hanging out together since first grade, playing baseball, football, hide-and-seek . . . just about everything we boys usually do. E. W.—that's what we call her—doesn't waste time with stupid stuff like makeup or lipstick or slumber parties. And she definitely doesn't spend hours every morning on her hair—E. W.'s hair is shorter than mine! Maybe if Keiko was more like E. W. I wouldn't mind being around her so much.

"I'd love to go," Keiko said, smiling up at Ben.

I felt the air escape from my lungs. I went inside the house to wash up, hoping that Keiko would change her mind.

33

5

She didn't change her mind. For three long hours Ben, Keiko, and I moped around the fairgrounds together. For me, the rides were more boring than ever, and poor Ben had to step in between Keiko and me every time we argued, which happened about every five minutes—on the Ferris wheel, in the shooting gallery, the haunted house—everywhere.

I could tell that Ben had had enough. After we bought a few sodas at a concession stand, Ben looked at his watch. "Well, it's

seven o'clock. We should probably get going soon."

I agreed, but there was one last thing I wanted to do. "I just want to say hi to Ronald," I said. Keiko smiled. I'm sure she liked the idea of being alone with Ben.

Ben narrowed his eyes. "You're not going to run away, are you?"

I forced a smile. "Promise."

I weaved through the thick crowd all the way to the far corner of the fairgrounds, where Ronald's booth was. A line of people stood in front of the booth, waiting for the wooden arrow to stop at their chosen name. Ronald wasn't there. I wasn't surprised. He usually left about four o'clock. But that's not why I went over there anyway. I wanted to look for the strange man I had seen the day before.

I searched the booths and stands in the area but he was nowhere to be found. That's

when I noticed another booth, in the far corner of the grounds, nestled under a canopy of needles from a pine tree.

There were no people huddled around this stand. As I approached the low table that acted as a counter, I realized there was nobody working there, either. The counter was crowded with odds and ends, junk mostly. There were small rocks, arrowheads, old photos of unfamiliar faces, small wooden boats, broken watches, tiny statues, and other objects that spilled over the table and covered the grass on the other side. A few feet back from the table, a wide sheet was hung like a curtain between two tree trunks. I wondered what was behind it.

"Hey, what did you find?" Ben's voice startled me. I had no idea how long he and Keiko had been standing behind me.

"Nothing," I said. "Just a bunch of junk."

"Is anybody here?" Keiko called out.

There was no response, and the three of us turned to leave when we heard something stirring behind the curtain.

I turned back around as a long, bony hand slowly parted the sheet and the old man I'd seen the day before appeared before us. He was wearing the same suit and tie, and he was staring at me, smiling. I thought my heart might explode in my chest.

"May I help you?" his voice was barely audible.

"No," replied Ben. "We're just looking, thanks."

"Very well," said the old man.

As he approached the counter, he lifted one hand to his face and began tickling his chin with long, yellow fingernails. He was looking right at me. "Is everything all right, young man?"

It was definitely him. No question about it. I took a deep breath.

"Y-yeah," I stammered. "It's just that . . . well, I think I saw you yesterday—"

"Well, of course you did. This is our third night in beautiful Dunmoore."

Keiko moved up beside me. "What do you mean 'our,'?" she asked.

The old man looked confused. "Oh, yes, of course. Let me introduce you to the lovely Ms. Sally . . . *Sally?*" he called.

A large black cat jumped up on the table, startling the three of us.

The man reached out and lifted the cat with one scrawny hand while he planted a kiss on the side of its head. "That's a good girl," he whispered.

I started looking over the junk again, hoping to find some old baseball cards or some other bargain. "What's that?" I asked, pointing to a large, opened box on the grass right beside the man. Overflowing from the box was what looked like a huge piece of yellow rubber.

"That wasn't there a minute ago," I said. I turned to Ben for confirmation, but he just shrugged his shoulders. "It wasn't," I insisted.

The old man's bulging eyes stared down at me. "I know a real thrill-seeker when I see one," he said. "You've chosen wisely." The man with the long white hair never turned to see what I was pointing at. "That," he whispered, "is a magic raft."

Ben's hand grabbed my shoulder. "Uh, I think we should probably get going."

"Wait, Ben," I said. "What do you mean, a 'magic raft'? What does it do?"

The old man leaned over and stuck his face in front of mine. "Do you know the Dunmoore River?"

I nodded.

"Paddle the raft under the old wooden bridge, and you will experience a ride more fantastic than anything you've ever dreamed of."

"Cool," I shouted. "How much does it cost?"

The man smiled. "For you, my friend, it will cost two dollars."

Ben nudged in between Keiko and me. "I really don't think—"

"Oh, come on, Ben. You said we could do something cool."

"Wait a second, Jack." Ben pulled me to one side and began to whisper. "You don't actually think this guy is for real, do you? I mean, come on—magic? Besides, I don't think Mom would want us taking some rubber raft out on the river. How do we know it's even safe?"

"Ben, you promised we'd go *swimming* in the river. If we take the raft out, we won't even get wet! Come on, Ben. You owe me one." I glanced over at Keiko.

My brother shook his head and grinned. "All right. We'll take the raft out on the river,

but just for a while. And Mom doesn't hear anything about this, right?"

"Deal," I said.

Ben turned back around and took out his monogrammed black leather wallet, a gift from Dad.

"Nice wallet," Keiko said. "But I can't believe you're actually going to buy that. . . . Although going out on the river sounds pretty cool."

"No, Ben," I snarled. "She's not—"

My brother closed his wallet emphatically. "If Keiko doesn't go, none of us goes."

I knew when I was beaten. I turned back to the junk dealer and smiled. "Thanks a lot, mister."

"The pleasure is mine." The box holding the yellow raft was already on the table. Beside it were two plastic oars and a small air pump. "I think you'll find these useful," the man said.

"How did those . . . never mind," I said, pulling the raft out of the box.

Ben handed the junk dealer two dollars and grabbed the oars. Keiko took the air pump.

"Oh, there's one more thing," the old man said. His bulging eyes bounced back and forth from me to Ben to Keiko. "Listen carefully, children. The raft is good for one ride only. If you take the raft out a second time, you will experience a world more terrifying than your worst nightmares." He smiled wickedly. "Very well. Good night."

We turned around and walked hurriedly away.

6

What a weirdo," Keiko said as we made our way through the crowded fairgrounds. "How can you possibly believe anything he said to you, Jack?"

I tried not to let Keiko bother me. Besides, I was getting excited thinking about taking the raft on the river. "Well," I began. "Of course I don't believe in magic. But isn't it cool that we got this raft for two dollars?"

"I can't believe we're doing this," Ben muttered ruefully. He checked his watch. "If we're going to do this, we have to get to the river soon. It's already seven o'clock. In an hour

it'll be dark, and we can't be on the river after dark."

When I reached the entrance—Ben and Keiko were lagging behind—a familiar voice rang out from behind the ticket booth. "Hey, Pierce," Arty Buller growled. "Where do you think *you're* going?"

Arty folded his arms across his chest as he stepped in front of me.

I tightened my grip on the raft. "What do you want, Buller?"

"I want whatever it is you're carrying, Pierce." His beady eyes had already locked onto the crumpled yellow heap tucked under my arm.

I moved back, but Arty's hands had already taken hold of the raft. I struggled to break his grip when he suddenly let go and backed up a step. "I'll get you, Pierce," Arty snickered. "Can't hide behind your brother forever."

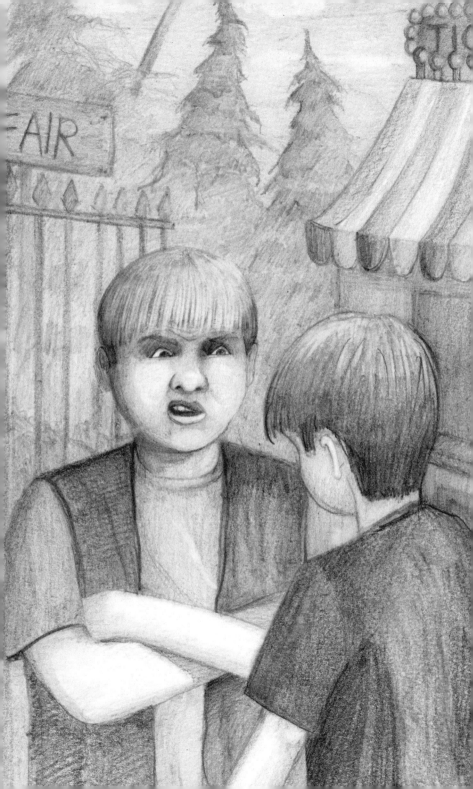

"You're pathetic, Buller," I called out to him as I walked through the exit line.

Arty must have seen Ben coming because he was gone by the time Ben and Keiko caught up with me. I saw his short blond hair sticking out from behind one of the portable toilets a few feet away. He seemed to be watching us.

I suddenly felt sorry for Arty. It was obvious he had nothing to do with himself. Maybe he just didn't like being at home. Then I remembered something Mom said about Arty's father. Mr. Buller was in the Gulf War. He was a tank driver or something—pretty awesome, huh? Well, we won that war, in case you didn't know, and Mr. Buller came back a hero and everything. But after some time he came down with a strange sickness and he couldn't work anymore. He just kind of hung around the house, getting sicker—and meaner—every day. That's all Mom knew.

I guess Arty just doesn't like going home.

Again I saw him peering at me from behind one of the white capsule-like toilets, but I pretended not to see him.

Ben, Keiko, and I stepped outside the fairgrounds. "Let's go through the woods across the street," I said. "We can reach the river in ten minutes."

"How far's the old bridge from there?" Keiko asked.

"It's been a while since I've been down there," Ben said. "I'd say it's no more than half an hour on the river."

We crossed the street and entered a narrow dirt path in the woods. There was still plenty of sunlight, so the going was easy. As I led the way through the woods, I thought about what the old man had said, about the bridge and everything else. It was all I could do to keep from running the rest of the way.

7

The sun was level with the tops of the trees when we arrived at the river. I had rushed Ben and Keiko every step of the way. I could barely wait any longer.

"It's getting dark already," Ben announced. He sat down on a fallen tree trunk and began pumping air into the raft. "I don't think this is such a good idea, Jack."

I sat down next to him. "It's the trees," I argued. "It only looks darker because the trees block out the sun." Of course, that was only partly true. The tall pines and poplars

that lined both sides of the river did block out the sun. But it was also getting dark—and fast.

I feared that Ben might change his mind if I didn't at least argue the point.

After Ben filled the raft with air, I helped him carry it down the bank of the river. Keiko followed with the oars.

I pushed aside a thick clump of reeds as Ben lowered the raft onto the surface of the water.

Where we set off from, the river was only about thirty feet across. In some places it was even narrower—more like a creek, really. Like our own private pool with fishes and plants and trees and animals all around. One time, a few years ago, when Jack and I were swimming in the river not far from our house, we saw a small bear drinking the water just a hundred feet down river. We watched quietly from behind

a tree, not wanting to scare it off—or make it angry. We never told Mom or Dad about the bear. It became a secret between Ben and me.

As I helped Ben push the front of the raft into the river, I tried not to think about how big the bear might have grown since then.

"It's going to be a tight fit," Ben said.

I looked at Keiko. "Well, maybe all of us shouldn't go."

"Get in," Ben said dryly. "And try not to get too much water in the raft."

My heart was racing. I must not have been paying attention, because when I lifted one foot into the raft, my other foot slipped and plunged into the dark water. Luckily I was wearing shorts, although my wet sneaker felt like a block of cement.

"Nice going," Keiko said. She was smiling mockingly.

Ben had to muffle a laugh.

I swung my waterlogged foot onto the raft and quickly moved to the front.

"Keiko, you're next," Ben said, helping her into the raft. "I'll sit in the back and paddle."

"There isn't much room in here," Keiko said, pushing her knees into my back.

I turned around and tried to look as serious as possible. "There's plenty of room on land, *Keeko*."

"Come on, guys," Ben yelled. "One more word and we're heading back."

We drifted quietly down river. Here and there bullfrogs groaned from small alcoves along the river's edge, and hungry blue gills broke the surface to snatch tiny bugs for dinner. Aside from Ben's slow, rhythmic rowing, all else was quiet.

After fifteen minutes or so, we rounded a bend in the river and the old bridge came into view.

I wondered if Ben or Keiko could hear how fast my heart was beating. Granted, none of us actually believed what the old man had said. I mean, how could a plastic raft be magic? But, then, what about the box at the old man's stand? How did it get to the table? And how did he know which item I wanted to see without looking? Then again, maybe I just imagined everything. I guess I just wanted some reason to believe the old man. And judging by the silence in the raft as we approached the old bridge, Ben and Keiko must have felt the same way.

8

The bridge looked much bigger up close. The river was wider here, maybe a hundred feet across, and the weathered old bridge seemed to hang no more than five feet over the surface of the river. The closer we got, the more convinced I was that we would have to duck as we went under. I'd seen the aging bridge several times when I was younger. Ben took me to a few ice hockey games during the winter, but back then the bridge was still open. Now it was closed.

Grass, weeds, trees, and the local wildlife had taken back the land.

As we floated under the bridge, the darkness seemed to swallow us up; it seemed to fold back on itself and become even darker and thicker, like a heavy, dense fog. It was so black, I couldn't see out the other side.

Ben lifted the oars out of the water and the raft slowed to a crawl.

"Whoa," Keiko said sarcastically. "Did you guys feel that?"

I knew she was kidding. It made me feel kind of foolish, because I was hoping against hope that something might happen. Keiko made me see how stupid I was being, and I hated her for it.

We waited almost a whole minute for something to happen but it never did. I felt like going back to the fair with the raft and giving that old man a piece of my

mind. Then I thought about how silly the whole thing was, and suddenly I didn't feel so angry.

"Well," Ben said. "At least we only paid two dollars." He dropped the oars in the water and began to paddle.

"What's that?" Keiko said, pointing down at the water next to the raft.

Ben leaned over the side of the raft. "It looks like bubbles," he replied.

I turned around and immediately saw what they were talking about. But it wasn't anything unusual, just air bubbles from a fish. "Let's go already," I said impatiently.

"Wait!" Keiko cried. "Look!"

Part of me didn't want to turn around again in case Keiko was just trying to be funny, but I couldn't help myself.

She wasn't kidding.

The bubbles had spread all around the raft. Before any of us could speak, the

sound of the erupting water filled our ears. I looked at Ben. His eyes and mouth were wide open. Behind me, Keiko was as stiff as a statue, her hands gripping the outer edge of the raft in panic.

I thought I should say something to calm them down. After all, whatever was happening beneath us was my fault.

"Don't worry," I yelled. "It's probably an underwater pipe. Nothing to—"

"Aaaaaaaaaaahhhhh!!"

Suddenly the raft tipped forward and plunged down at a sharp angle. I shut my eyes and mouth and gripped the rope on both sides of the raft, expecting to be submerged in the water at any moment.

Keiko clung to my back in fear. "W-h-a-t'-s h-a-p-p-e-n-i-n-g?"

Water splashed up at us, but it felt like we were going down a tunnel, not under the water.

Suddenly, the raft sped up. We must have been going eighty miles per hour! The force pushed Keiko and me into Ben's lap.

"H-o-l-d o-n!" Ben screamed.

Then, as quickly as it had started, it stopped. The water surface beneath us leveled off, and the raft drifted slowly forward on a weak current. Everything was quiet except for our heavy breathing. It sounded like the three of us had just finished running wind sprints.

I parted the fingers on the hand covering my eyes.

We were still in some kind of a dark tunnel, but a strong white light streamed in from an opening ahead of us.

"Are we alive?" Keiko asked in a quavering voice.

"I don't know how, but it sure feels like it." Ben said.

I became aware of something very strange about this place. It was like the air I

breathed—and the feeling of it on my skin—was somehow so perfect, I hardly noticed it at all. My whole body felt as light as a feather. "Do you guys feel any different?" I asked.

"Yeah," Keiko replied. "It's weird. It's kind of like the air is flowing right through me. Maybe the old man was telling the truth!" Suddenly there was a loud splash to our left, and Keiko gave an ear-splitting scream.

"What's happened?" Ben asked.

Keiko looked terrified. "Something just jumped out of the water! I—I think it was a . . . porpoise?"

"There it is!" Ben cried. "In front of us!"

I didn't believe it until I saw it for myself: Not one, but two porpoises, diving in and out of the water in front of the raft. Only these were not your average porpoises.

"Look," Ben said. "You can see right through them!"

Keiko was practically standing in the raft. "It's like they're made of glass!"

"I think they're leading us out of the tunnel," I said.

"Yeah, but leading us where?" Ben asked.

All three of us were leaning forward, too excited to speak, when the raft finally emerged from the tunnel into a narrow river.

"Cool!" I cried. "Look at the water. You can see all the way to the bottom!"

Keiko was shading her eyes. "Where's that light coming from?"

I craned my neck to see. The strange white light shone down from somewhere high above, but a wall of lush vegetation that surrounded the river—plants and trees greener and thicker than anything I'd ever seen—blocked out its source, which seemed to be coming from the sky off to our left. The peculiar light made it seem neither like day nor night, but somewhere in between—kind

of like living in the glow of a lightning strike, if that makes any sense.

In the distance, I heard what sounded like the rush of a waterfall. All around us birds chirped from hidden spots among the bushes and trees. I was so excited, it must have looked like my eyes were popping out of my head.

In front of us, the glass porpoises continued to lead the way.

"This isn't the Dunmoore River anymore, is it?" Ben said, jokingly.

No it isn't, came a soft voice from above.

I turned quickly in my seat. "Who said that?"

Ben and Keiko were already looking up at the sky, when, suddenly, the river dipped a few feet, just as the raft rounded a sharp bend. Straight ahead of us, just above the tops of the trees, was a huge silver moon. I asked Ben and Keiko, "You guys heard that,

didn't you?" They both quietly nodded, still looking at the moon.

Welcome to Noit-ani-gami, a world where your fantasies come true!

Silence filled the small raft.

I could almost feel my hair standing on end. It sounded like the voice was coming from the moon itself!

Since my brother and Keiko had stopped moving altogether, I thought I should at least try to say something back to whoever was talking to us. "Who are you? *Where* are you?"

I am right before you.

"Well, all I see is the moon, and everyone knows the moon doesn't—"

It is not important what you think you know. Now you must prepare for your first adventure. And remember, make sure and stay on the raft.

"You can speak," I said.

In the back of the raft, Ben cleared his throat and leaned forward. "Exactly . . . what adventure?" he asked, sounding just a little embarrassed.

I believe Keiko can answer that.

But there wasn't time to ask Keiko, because something else had grabbed our attention. About a hundred feet ahead, splashing tons of water on the river, was an immense waterfall.

"Ben," I yelled. "What should we do?"

Ben quickly took up the oars, but the current had already picked up too much speed. There wasn't enough time to row to the shore. The crushing sound of the water-fall grew louder every second, until we could feel sprinkles of water splashing up from the force. I crawled backward, pushing up against Keiko, who was covering her eyes with her hands.

"We have to jump," Ben yelled.

"But . . . the voice said not to leave the raft," Keiko remembered.

Suddenly the bottom of the raft began to lift above the surface of the water, first only a few inches, then it became a few feet.

"What's happening?" I yelled over the pounding force of the water.

"Stay down!" Ben warned.

The sound of the falls grew louder, but the water never hit us. I waited a few more seconds, then lifted my head from my lap and looked out.

"Hey, guys," I said in a trembling voice. "You're not going to believe this. We're flying!" I looked back for the moon, but it had vanished.

The raft had risen straight up over the waterfall and was hovering high in the air. I held the ropes tightly and looked over the side. The river snaked for miles through the tall trees.

"I can't believe this," Keiko said excitedly. "I've always wanted to fly!"

The raft flew straight over the river, dipping, then soaring back up. My hair flew back and the wind made my eyes tear but the feeling was incredible. And even though we were high up in the air, in a tiny plastic raft, I was somehow sure that we were all safe. I looked back at Ben. "Isn't this great?"

My brother smiled, then nodded. "Just don't look down."

I knew Ben was looking out for me, but really—what would flying be without looking down? I sneaked a glance at the river below. It was incredibly beautiful—the clear water surrounded by the greenest plants and trees I'd ever seen. And directly below the raft, the two crystal porpoises dived in and out of the water in perfect formation.

"When I was a little girl growing up in Japan," Keiko yelled above the rushing wind,

RAFTERS

"I used to dream of flying over the river that ran through the mountains above our house." She looked over the side of the raft, and a tear formed in the corner of her eye. "It looked just like this."

After a few minutes the raft slowly began to descend.

"Everybody stay low and hold on tight," Ben said.

We gently touched down on the calm surface of the river. For a few moments none of us knew what to say—it's not often you speak to the moon, and find out what it's like to fly.

"The moon was right," Keiko said. "Your dreams and adventures really do come true here." She turned and looked at Ben. "Do you have an adventure you've always wanted to experience?"

Before Ben could answer, the water all around us suddenly began to churn and

froth, and the raft violently rocked back and forth.

"I think I might regret it now," Ben said. "But I've always wanted to go white-water rafting! Hang on!"

Suddenly we were hurdling down the river at full speed, water splashing in our faces and soaking our clothes. Huge gray boulders shot up out of nowhere, but Ben steered us safely past every one of them.

"This is awesome!" Ben cried.

I have to be honest, it was a little scary sitting in front. The tip of the raft bounced up and down on the hard surface. I got the worst of it. By the time the current slowed to its normal pace, my hair and shirt were drenched.

An inch of water lay at the bottom of the raft. I turned around to see how the others had taken it. They, too, were soaking wet; although Ben didn't seem to mind. He had a wide grin on his face.

"I've never imagined it would be that much fun," he exclaimed, his chest heaving from the excitement.

As we continued floating down river, a strange quiet settled over the raft. I could tell what Ben and Keiko were thinking. They were wondering what *my* fantasy was. Maybe they were too frightened to ask. The truth was, I was kind of afraid to find out myself. I couldn't imagine what it might be.

We approached a dark bend in the river. The vegetation was even thicker than before, and the tops of the towering trees seemed to interlock overhead, blocking out most of the moonlight. A strange feeling coursed through my body. My skin began to tingle. It was almost like a part of me knew what to expect.

Everything looked normal as we rounded the bend. There were no waterfalls, no rocky water, and no crystal dolphins. There was only a clearing along the bank of the river to

our left. As the raft drifted closer, I could see the outline of something—or someone—in the middle of the clearing, but a large branch from an overhanging tree blocked the view.

"Jack, Keiko, better watch out for the branches," Ben warned.

His voice was tense and anxious.

The closer we got, the clearer the figure became. It was a man, standing alone on the bank of the river. My heart began to pound so hard I was sure Ben and Keiko could hear it.

"Dad!" I cried.

My father stood by the edge of the water. Tall and thin, his pale face was framed by thick dark hair that fell crookedly over his forehead. It was exactly how I remembered him. Tears welled up in my eyes. This was *my* wish, and there he was. As I looked at Dad, practically every memory I had of him came flooding back to me.

He was waving to us and smiling as the raft pulled alongside of him. I wanted to say something to my dad, I wanted to tell him I loved him, but the words got caught in my throat. I could hear Ben crying quietly behind me. He put his hand on my shoulder and squeezed gently.

I stood up.

"Jack!" Ben yelled. He pushed by Keiko and stood up, grabbing me by the shirt and pushing me back into my seat. "Are you crazy, Jack? He's not real!"

"Let me go!" I tried to stand back up, but Ben held my shoulders down. "I need to talk to him, Ben! I never even said good-bye to him. Please—I just need to—"

"No, Jack! We're not supposed to get out of the raft!"

Ben was standing next to me on the edge of the raft, holding me with one hand and wiping the tears from his eyes with the other.

None of us ever saw the branch.

It seemed to come out of nowhere, suddenly striking Ben on the shoulder and knocking him into the river. Keiko and I were stunned. It took a few seconds before we realized what had happened. But it was too late. The current had strengthened, pulling us further down river and spinning our raft around. We were now at least fifty feet away from where Ben had fallen in.

"Ben!" I screamed, scanning the water behind us for any sign of him. It seemed like an hour went by before I finally spotted him swimming toward the river bank. I felt a rush of relief. At least he was okay.

Keiko, who was now facing forward, reached back and grabbed my shoulder. "Jack—" She never finished her sentence.

When I turned around, I realized why she was so frightened. The river ended just a few

feet ahead of us—and neither one of us had heard the roaring waterfall, which now seemed deafeningly loud.

Keiko and I looked at each other with grim faces, then we both lay down and covered our eyes as the raft went over the falls.

9

For the second time in one day I thought my life had ended. But the fact that my entire body was soaking wet told me otherwise.

After we fell over the waterfall, we had entered a dark tunnel, kind of like the one we passed through at the beginning of the trip. Somehow we ended up right where we began, near the fallen log on the Dunmoore River.

Only now Ben was gone.

Keiko and I were still lying on the bottom of the raft, in three inches of water. I pried my hands from my eyes and sat up. It was

dark and quiet, and a damp feeling of dread had seeped into my bones. I had to figure out a way to find Ben.

"Are you okay?" I asked.

"Yeah," she mumbled. "I think so." She sat up slowly. "How did we get here?"

I took up the oars and began to paddle toward shore. "I don't know, but I have an idea who might."

"Let me guess," Keiko said. "We're going back to the fair?"

"*We're* not going anywhere," I said.

"What?"

Considering all the trouble I was about to go through—*what was I going to tell Mom?!* —I figured it was best to rid myself of Keiko now instead of later. I jumped off the raft and turned to give her a hand. She ignored me and stomped up the river bank.

Struggling, I dragged the raft up to the tree trunk. "Look," I said. "It's not just that

we don't like each other. It's more compli-cated than that."

"What are you talking about, Jack?" Keiko walked right up to my face. I'd never seen her so angry. "And don't tell me that I don't like you," she yelled, "just to justify your feelings toward me!" I opened my mouth but nothing came out, which was probably good, because I was still trying to figure out what she meant. I sat down on the log.

"Look," Keiko said. "Ben is your brother, but he's my friend, too. And I feel partially responsible for what happened, so I think its only right that I help find him."

"*You* feel responsible? How do you think *I* feel? My brother is gone and we might never find him—and it's all my fault! Not yours. *I* pressured him into buying the raft in the first place." I dropped my head into my hands. "I can't believe this is happening."

Keiko sat down next to me. "We'll find him, Jack. I know we will. If he's still alive, and I'm sure he is, we'll do everything we can to bring him back. But we have to help each other."

Keiko was right. If we had any chance of finding Ben, we'd have to do it together. There was no way of knowing what we might be up against. "We have to go back," I said. "Back through the tunnel."

"But what about the old man's warning? Don't you remember what he said about going a second time? You know, a 'nightmare world'?"

"Do you have any better suggestions?"

Keiko stared at the ground. "Maybe we should go to the police."

"No! Do you think they'd believe our story? I mean, a flying raft? They'd probably arrest us."

"You're right."

I stood up and dragged the raft into the nearby bushes. "I have a plan that might work, but I'll have to leave my house early if it's going to work. Can you meet me here tomorrow morning at seven?"

Keiko nodded. "No problem. I'll tell my grandparents that I'll be at my friend Sue's house. I can sneak back in through my bedroom window if we get back late."

"Cool. Now let's visit our friend, the junk dealer, before we go home. It's a little out of the way, but he might be able to answer a few questions."

Everything had happened so fast, there wasn't time to think about Ben or the strange land we had passed through. *What had the moon's voice called it, Noit-ani-gami? I'd have to think about that later.*

When we started down the path in the woods toward the fair, we heard a loud rustling in the bushes.

"What was that?" Keiko whispered.

I waited a few seconds, but the forest remained quiet. "It was probably nothing," I said. "Maybe a raccoon or a skunk. Let's go."

As we headed off through the woods, we never saw the bulky figure scuttle out from behind a tree and run off in the opposite direction.

10

From the woods, the fairgrounds were a huge mass of lights and moving bodies. Keiko and I crossed the street, weaved through the parking lot, and headed for the ticket booth.

"Wait," I said. "I've got a better idea." Keiko followed me around the corner to a portion of the fence that was hidden in shadows. A two-foot section of the fence had been cut from the bottom up.

I got on my knees and pulled one of the steel flaps toward me.

Keiko put her hands on her hips. "Jack, what are you doing?"

"Sorry," I muttered. "But I'm a little shy in the wallet."

Keiko sighed. "Well, since I only have a dollar, and the tickets are five dollars each . . . But we *will* pay them back later, okay?"

"Okay, okay."

We crawled through the opening of the fence, crept through the dark alley between the shooting gallery and the fortune teller booth, and came out into the bright light of the main fairway.

The crowds were thick, and Keiko and I bumped into many shoulders on our way to the far corner of the fairgrounds.

"Do you think he'll be able to tell us how to find Ben?" Keiko asked anxiously.

"He better," I replied. "Or else."

The truth is, I didn't know what "or else" meant. I only knew that the old junk dealer

better do whatever he could to help us find my brother.

We passed Ronald's spinning wheel booth. I glanced over but Ronald wasn't there, although at that very moment a young girl was leaving the booth carrying a huge stuffed rabbit.

We knew we were getting close when the crowds began to thin out.

I sprinted the last few feet and came to a sudden stop. The booth was gone.

Keiko ran up behind me. "Where is it?" she asked, out of breath. "He couldn't have just disappeared."

We walked under the trees where the table and the curtain and the old junk dealer had been, but there was no trace of anything.

"This is too creepy," Keiko said. "Should we look around for him?"

"Something tells me we won't find him here. Or maybe anywhere."

Keiko frowned and looked at her watch. "Well, it's almost nine-thirty. What time do you have to be home?"

Then I remembered: Mom said she might be home by ten o'clock! "I have to go," I yelled. "I'll see you tomorrow morning, by the river, at seven o'clock."

I didn't hear Keiko say good-bye. My mind was racing with troubles that lay ahead. Ben was lost in some bizarre world known only to Keiko and me, and Mom could not find out. I turned sideways and speared my way through the crowd, heading for the tear in the fence.

11

The house appeared dark from the back-yard. Just to be safe, I walked around the side and peeked through one of the garage windows: Mom's car was still gone.

But time was running out. I unlocked the front door and ran straight into the kitchen. The house was as hot as a furnace. Sweat dripped down my forehead and cheeks as I ran around the living room opening all the windows.

I took out a pencil and a sheet of paper from a drawer in the kitchen and sat down

to write. The clock above the oven read 9:55. Mom could be home at any minute.

When I finished my letter, I laid it in the center of the table and quickly re-read it just to make sure I'd covered everything.

Dear Mom,

   Ben and I went to sleep early.
   We ate at the fair, so don't worry.
   Tomorrow morning we'll be getting up early to go fishing down by the river. You probably won't see us until tomorrow night.
   Have a good day at work.

Love, Jack

I ran upstairs. In the hallway closet I took out several blankets and promptly stuffed them under Ben's bed sheet, doing my best to mold them into the shape of a body. I was

almost finished when I heard a car pull into our driveway. With no time to waste, I pulled my sneakers off, shut out the light, and jumped onto the top bunk.

The front door creaked open. A minute later, I heard Mom's footsteps climbing up the staircase. I glanced down at Ben's bed to make sure everything was in order and noticed that a bright purple blanket, Ben's right leg, had come out of the sheet and was dangling onto the floor.

I was about to jump down and repair the leg when the door swung open.

With my sheet pulled up to my eyes, I peeked at the doorway and saw Mom looking in. I waited for her to go, but she just stood there, staring. Suddenly she lifted a hand. I thought I saw her reach for the light switch on our wall. *Busted,* I thought. I heard a click and closed my eyes, expecting Mom to rush in.

Instead the hall light went off, and Mom retreated to her bedroom.

I tried to slow my breathing. The first half of my plan was complete. Now all I had to do was wait for Mom to be asleep, then set Ben's alarm for six o'clock. Ben always got up before Mom. Tomorrow morning, I would, too.

12

When I arrived at the river the next morning, Keiko was already there, sitting on the log.

She stood up. "Is everything okay?"

"Yeah. I got out before my mom woke up."

Keiko heaved a sigh of relief and together we walked over to the raft and pulled it out from under the bushes. We were dragging it down to the water when we heard something stirring back by the log.

"Shhh." Keiko put a hand up, signaling me to stop. She pointed to a fat tree trunk.

At the base of the tree, I saw a red high-top sneaker peeking out beside a knotted root. "Who's there?" I called out.

There was more movement, then a head popped out from behind the tree. Arty Buller's head.

"What are you doing here, Buller?" I asked in a gruff voice.

Arty grinned and lumbered down the river bank. "The question is, what are you doing here, Pierce?"

I shot a glance at Keiko, who was looking at the ground.

"What exactly do you want?" I asked.

Arty smiled. "I want to go with you."

"No way," Keiko snarled.

Arty put his hands on his hips. "I know all about Ben. I heard the whole thing last night."

"So it was you snooping around," Keiko said.

"Yeah, it was me. And if you don't want anybody going to the police, or telling a certain someone's mother, you'd be smart and take me along with you."

"Sounds like he's got us," Keiko whispered.

"Arty, you don't know what you're getting into," I said.

"Look, I don't know exactly what's going on here, but I figure, it sounds kind of cool, and, I don't know, maybe I can help out. I mean, your brother's always been kind of cool to me anyway."

From that moment on I saw Arty in a slightly different light. He was still a bully, but a part of him seemed genuinely concerned about Ben. Besides, I didn't really have a choice.

"All right, you can come. But you're rowing,"

"Why me?" Arty grumbled as he stepped into the raft.

Keiko and I looked at one another and shook our heads as we boarded the raft.

"So, where are we going, anyway?" Arty asked.

"Well," said Keiko, "we bought this magic raft from a strange old man at the fair, who said we would have the ride of our lives if we just paddled the raft under the old wooden bridge. We did, and we found out the raft was magic, only Ben fell off before the ride ended. Now we're going back to find Ben even though the old man told us not to take the raft out a second time. Does that make sense?"

Arty narrowed his eyes. "Yeah, right. I'm sorry I asked."

"She's telling the truth, Arty."

"We'll see," Arty mumbled to himself.

13

When we reached the dark beneath the bridge, Arty pulled the oars out of the water. "I guess this is where we sink into some other planet," he said sarcastically.

"It's not another planet," Keiko fired back.

"Whatever," Arty snickered.

But Arty certainly wasn't snickering for long, because seconds later the water around us began to bubble, and once again the raft plunged into the mysterious darkness that would hopefully lead us to Ben.

Arty was silent by the time the raft leveled off and entered what seemed to be a dark tunnel. We were all soaking wet from the ride down.

I looked nervously at Keiko. Unlike the last ride, there was no white light coming from the opening up ahead.

"What's going on?" Arty asked. His voice was trembling.

"I'm not sure," I replied. "But we're about to find out."

We were out of the tunnel.

First I became aware of a strange crimson glow all around us. The creepy reddish light came from above. I looked up and saw the moon, huge like in the first ride, with one awful difference: This moon was blood-red!

"Oh, no!" I cried.

"What is it?" Keiko asked. Her fingers were digging into my shoulder blade like a pitchfork.

I turned around and saw that both Keiko and Arty had their hands over their eyes. I said, "Just open your eyes and see for yourself. And remember that all of this is probably not real, just some sort of scary illusion or something."

The crimson moon was the only source of light. But it was bright enough to illuminate most everything around us, even though it was dark. I kind of wished that I hadn't looked at all.

The trees that lined the river on both sides were now lifeless, with gnarled, bony branches that reached out over the water like giant claws. The same awful trees stretched back from the banks of the river for as far as the eye could see.

The raft drifted slowly through the murky water. Suddenly, a horrifying howl echoed in the distance. It sounded like the cry of the living dead.

"Okay, where are we? What's going on?" Arty's voice was quavering.

I could feel Keiko's body shivering against my back, even though the temperature in this terrible place must have been at least ninety degrees.

"The old man was right," Keiko said. "We should never have come back a second time. Never!"

"She's right," Arty agreed. "I say we turn back now."

"But we have to find Ben!" I shouted.

I was scanning both sides of the river when I heard a strange buzzing sound coming from above. The sound soon became so loud, it made my teeth rattle. "Does anybody hear that?" I asked.

Keiko was the first to respond. "Oh my—"

"What's wrong?" I demanded.

"It—it's on your head," Keiko stammered. "It's a giant mosquito!"

I rolled my eyes upward and immediately I could see the long spindly black legs, each longer than a foot, perched right above my forehead. "Ahhhhhhh! Make it go away! Please, make it go away! I hate mosquitoes!"

Keiko took one of the oars and waved it at the creature. As big as a television set, the huge insect flew up into the blood-red sky. Then another one swooped down over us. And another. Luckily Keiko was able to keep them away by swinging the oar.

I looked up and saw a nightmarish sight: A huge swarm of the giant creatures was passing over us. The buzzing was so loud we had to cover our ears.

"Let me guess," Keiko said. "Mosquitoes are your worst fear?"

I shrugged and nodded. "Just let me know when you see them again."

As I sat up I noticed that Arty's face was as pale as a sheet. "What's wrong with you?"

He was pointing just ahead of us, where something was rising from the murky surface of the water.

"What is it?" Keiko asked, biting her nails.

I leaned forward. "If I'm not mistaken, I'd say it was . . . a claw."

In a moment two claws emerged, followed by a skull with glowing eye sockets. Then another of the ghastly creatures emerged from the water. Soon there were twenty, maybe thirty of the ghoulish beasts.

I turned to Arty. "Do you know what we're looking at, Arty?"

Arty was already standing. He looked like he was about to cry. "It—it's the boogeyman!" he wailed. If I hadn't been so terrified, I would have laughed.

Before Keiko or I could stop him, Arty jumped into the river behind the raft and began swimming desperately for shore. Some of the creatures turned and started

trudging after him, but it looked like Arty would at least make it to shore.

"Quick, Jack, let's row to the other side before one of those . . . things gets us."

"I agree," I said as I moved to the back of the raft and began paddling.

When we reached shore, we noticed that a few of the horrible zombie-looking creatures were staggering around. None of them had seen us.

Further up the bank, there were some large rock formations and what looked like the mouth of a cave.

"Let's go up there," I said. "Maybe if we wait in that cave a while they'll go away. Then we can come back down and look for Arty and Ben."

Keiko nodded, and we climbed quickly up the craggy incline, looking over our shoulders every step of the way.

14

We made our way into the small cave and stopped just inside the opening. For a few minutes we stood there catching our breath. Finally Keiko spoke. "Do you think it's safe in here?"

"I don't know. At least safer than out there, for now." I could barely see Keiko, but I could feel her standing right next to me. She must have been as scared as I was.

"Jack, in case something happens to us—"

"No, Keiko, don't say that. We're going to be okay. We're going to find Ben, and we're

going to get out of here." I'd never seen Keiko nervous like this before, and I felt kind of bad for her.

"Well, anyway," Keiko said, "I didn't get a chance to tell you before . . . I thought it was really nice about your dad. About him being your wish and everything. I'm glad you got to see him again."

With everything that had happened on this second ride, I had almost forgotten about seeing Dad. Suddenly everything I had felt when I saw him came rushing back to me, and I was afraid I might cry again. I was glad it was too dark for Keiko to see me.

I sniffled. "You know, the thing is, Ben and my mom always talk about him, but I never even *thought* about him. And whenever I did, I couldn't even remember what he looked like at all. It was just this blank face, you know?" Tears were running down my face now.

Keiko took my hand in hers. She nodded.

"I felt really guilty about not remembering him," I continued, "until I saw him standing there. And then I realized that I *did* remember him, I must have, because that was *my* fantasy." I didn't know if I was making any sense to Keiko, but I didn't care. It felt good just to talk about it.

"I'm happy for you, Jack," Keiko said softly. I could tell she meant it. For once she wasn't being sarcastic.

"Thanks," I said, and I smiled at her. I couldn't tell if she saw it in the dark.

"Do you think Arty's okay?" Keiko asked suddenly.

"I don't know. I mean, those boogeyman creatures were pretty scary . . ."

"So were the mosquitoes," Keiko said. "I was afraid they were going to carry us away or something, or suck out all our blood!" I was expecting Keiko to laugh, to make fun of

me for being afraid of something as stupid as mosquitoes, but she didn't. I had to hand it to her for that.

"Keiko, we've only seen my fear and Arty's so far. We haven't had yours yet, have we? I mean, assuming it's not being stuck in a cave with me."

Keiko chuckled. "No, that's not it."

"What is it then?" The way I figured it, we still had one more nightmare to deal with, and we were better off knowing what to expect ahead of time.

Keiko grew quiet. Even in the dark, I could tell she was getting scared again by the way she was breathing. "Come on, Keiko, what is it? You need to tell me."

"Well," she began, her voice shaking slightly, "when I lived in Japan—"

Slam!

"What was that?" I shouted. Only a few feet behind us, a huge boulder had come

crashing down from the cave wall, slamming into the ground and sending a cloud of dust into the air. Then another chunk of rock came tumbling down, followed by some smaller pieces, and more dust.

"Oh, no . . ." Keiko said.

"What? What's happening?" I asked.

Suddenly the ground under my feet shifted, and a loud rumbling filled the cave. Then everything began to shake, and rocks started falling from every direction. Keiko and I looked at each other.

"*Earthquake!*" we shouted.

The ground between us began to split open, and before I even realized what was happening, a giant crack appeared and snaked its way along the floor of the cave. I tried to step away from the crack—which was becoming wider by the second—but the floor was shaking so much that I lost my balance.

I tumbled backward, into the wall behind me. Small rocks cascaded down from the roof of the cave. I bent my head down and covered it with my hands for protection. Everything was shaking so hard I was sure the whole cave was about to collapse on top of me.

I heard an ear-splitting scream.

Keiko! I'd completely lost sight of her when the ground ripped apart, and the shaking and dust made it impossible to see anything. What had happened to her?

Suddenly the quaking stopped as quickly as it had begun. An eerie silence settled over the cave. I wiped the dust out of my eyes and squinted into the darkness.

Keiko was gone.

15

"Keiko? Keiko, where are you?" I got to my feet and walked slowly to the edge of the black pit that had formed in the middle of the cave. I heard a soft moan coming from below. "Keiko?" I peered over the edge into the pit. I could barely make out Keiko's outline. She was at least ten feet down, lying on her side, wedged between jagged walls of earth on either side.

Before I even had time to think about it, I was climbing down into the pit. Luckily the incline wasn't too steep. I slowly made my

way to the bottom and crouched down next to her.

"Keiko?" I poked her shoulder softly, but she didn't respond. Even in the dark I could see a long, bloody gash stretching across her forehead. Keiko was in serious trouble! I had to get her out of there somehow, get her back to the real world and get help, even if it meant abandoning my search for Ben for the time being. I'd already lost Ben and Arty to this place, and I wasn't about to leave Keiko there, alone and hurt.

I pulled her up into a half-sitting, half-standing position and balanced her against the wall. Then I scrambled up and out of the hole. Lying down flat on the ground, I leaned over the edge and reached into the pit for Keiko's arms, pulling as hard as I could and lifting her until she was close enough for me to grab her around the waist. I heaved with all my might, and finally pulled Keiko out of the pit.

Struggling to catch my breath, I picked up Keiko and walked to the opening of the cave. The raft was still sitting where we had left it on the bank. Somehow I had to get us down there, onto the river, and over the waterfall, which I assumed was not too far. I looked both ways. The coast was clear.

Beneath the red light of the moon, Keiko looked even worse than I had feared. *I'm sorry, Ben,* I thought. *I promise I'll come back and find you.*

I made a break for the raft. I couldn't move any faster than a walk—at least not while carrying Keiko, who was practically the same size as me. Suddenly I heard a low moan coming from a distance away. I recognized the sound immediately. The creatures with the glowing eyes! I looked over my shoulder, and sure enough, three of the creatures, arms outstretched, were heading straight for us! They were still pretty far

away, but they were moving a lot faster than Keiko and I were moving.

Finally, when they were so close I could almost feel their fingers brushing against my back, we reached the raft. I practically threw Keiko into it and jumped in after her, pushing the raft away from the shore at the same time. I grabbed the oars and paddled frantically toward the middle of the river. When I felt safe enough to look back, I saw the three creatures on the bank staring after us, eyes blazing.

"Jack? What happened?" Keiko was sitting up, rubbing her head and frowning.

"Keiko, thank God! Are you okay?"

"I don't know, I think so. What's going on?"

"Um, just a close call, that's all. We have to get you home."

"Home? But what about Ben?"

"Don't worry about that right now, Keiko. I'll have to come back for him."

"How do you know you can get back here at all? The old man at the fair only mentioned two rides . . ."

"We'll find out soon enough."

"We?" Keiko asked, smiling.

"Well, I guess I *could* use your help . . . I have to find Ben. No matter what it takes. But right now the important thing—oh my God, look!"

On the far side of the bank stood a fourth zombie. It was wearing red high-top sneakers.

Keiko gasped. "Those are Arty's shoes!"

"Let's get out of here!" I shouted, and paddled furiously toward the end of the river, where the waterfall would take us out of this horrible world.

As we got closer I noticed a figure in the distance, running along the shore in our direction. *Probably another creature,* I thought. "Lie down and try to stay still," I told Keiko. She wasn't listening.

"Jack!" she said, squinting at the approaching figure. "That's Arty!"

Sure enough, it was Arty, waving his arms wildly and yelling to us. "You have to swim for it!" we shouted. He was holding something in his hand, which he then shoved into his pocket.

"Hurry!" I screamed. The current was beginning to pull us toward the waterfall, which we could now see and hear. There wasn't much time.

Arty was halfway to the raft when one of the creatures surfaced in the black water next to him.

"Arty! Look out!" I screamed. The creature reached a hand out of the water and was about to rake its razor-sharp claw over Arty's back when I pulled him into the raft by his shirt. He fell in a wet heap next to Keiko.

"We thought you were dead! Those creatures had your shoes, and—"

"They must've picked them up or something. I took 'em off after I swam to shore because they were so wet. Anyway, look what I found on the ground—"

In his hand was a black water-logged wallet.

It was Ben's.

"That means he's alive. Doesn't it?" Keiko asked.

"Yeah, I hope so," I exclaimed. "Thanks, Arty." I didn't know what finding Ben's wallet actually meant, but just looking at it made me feel better. I prayed that he was safe.

"You guys! Hang on!" Keiko shrieked. I turned back toward the front of the raft. We were only a few feet from the edge of the waterfall.

The raft started to pitch violently forward. "Aaaahhhhhh!" we screamed in unison. I closed my eyes and hung on.

epilogue

The police officer paced back and forth across our living room floor. I was sitting on our old overstuffed green sofa next to Mom, who was drying her eyes with a tissue. Outside, the sun was setting beyond the wall of trees in our backyard.

The officer was tall, with a stomach that spilled over his belt. He stared at a small note pad in his hand. "So," he said in a husky voice, "let me go over this one more time. Your son has been missing since yesterday afternoon, correct?"

Mom sniffled and nodded to the officer.

"And you, Jack, were the last person to see him?"

I moved to the edge of the sofa, straightened my back, and folded my hands. It's not often you find yourself making up stories to tell to a police officer. I wanted to look as respectable as I possibly could.

"Yeah," I said. "After we went fishing yesterday, Ben said he wanted to be alone for a while. He told me that he would meet me home later." I stared at the shiny pair of handcuffs dangling from the officer's hip. "But I'm sure he's fine, officer. He's just had a lot of pressure lately. I'm sure he'll be back soon, really."

It didn't sound very convincing, but at least it made Mom feel a little better. The officer pursed his lips. "Okay, Mrs. Pierce. We'll do everything we can. You try to get some rest."

Mom walked the officer to the front door, thanked him, then walked up the staircase. I heard her bedroom door close.

I pushed aside the curtain on the window and watched the police car pull away.

Suddenly a tapping sound came from the back door. I rushed to the back of the house and pushed open the screen door. Keiko and Arty were standing against the back wall of the house like two burglars. Keiko was holding a heavy-duty flashlight. Arty wore a sleeveless T-shirt and a headband.

"Are you guys ready?" I asked, quietly shutting the door.

Keiko and Arty nodded, and the three of us crept through the backyard to the path in the woods.

I didn't know where the next ride would take us, but I knew my brother was still alive, and that he was waiting for me to take him home.

Will Jack, Keiko, and Arty ever find Ben?

What mysteries will their future adventures hold?

Will they discover the identity of the strange junk dealer?

Learn the answers to these and other questions in:

Rafters #2, Keeper of the River